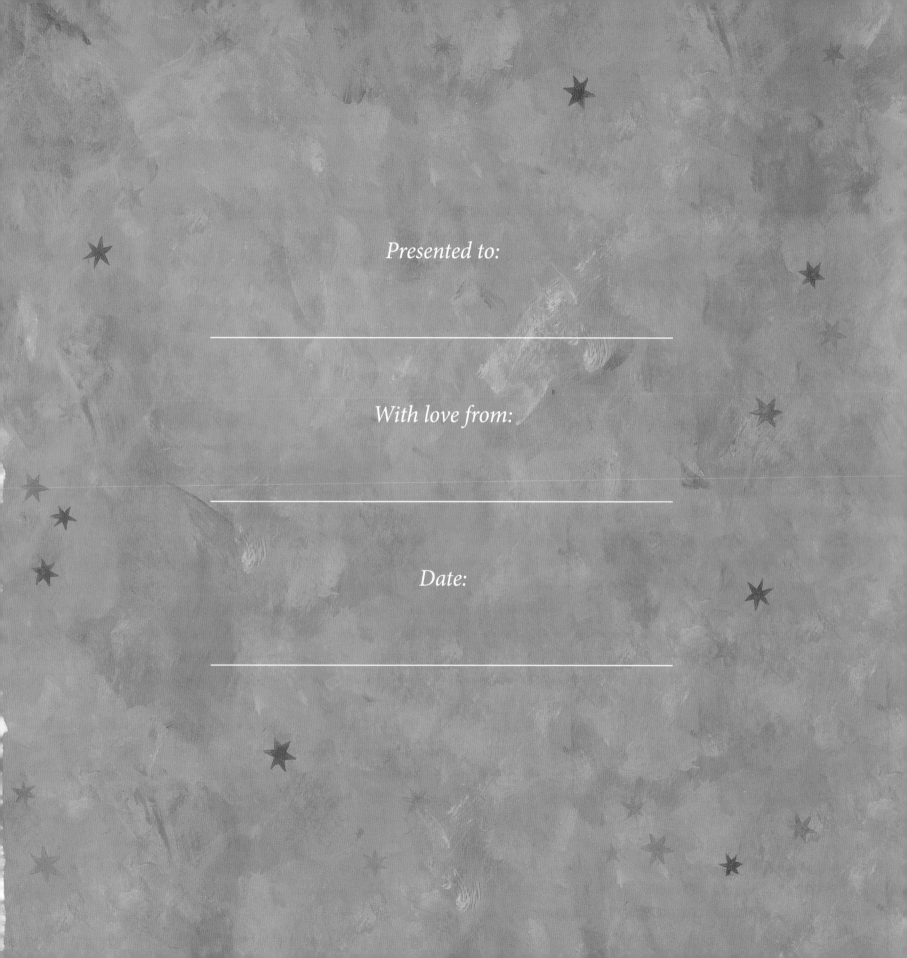

Presented to:

_____

With love from:

_____

Date:

_____

For Steven, my eldest son,
in memory of the day you were born, when:

It felt as if my love took flight
And soared into the air,
And joined creation's welcome song
As you were lying there.

Love, Mum
–GN

À ma maman — to my mom.

–AB

ZONDERKIDZ

The Wonder That Is You
Copyright © 2019 by Glenys Nellist
Illustrations © 2019 by Aurelie Blanz

Requests for information
should be addressed to:

Zonderkidz, 3900 *Sparks Dr. SE,*
Grand Rapids, Michigan 49546

Library of Congress Cataloging-in-Publication Data

Names: Nellist, Glenys, 1959- author.
   Title: The wonder that is you / by Glenys Nellist.
Description: Grand Rapids, Michigan : Zonderkidz, [2019] | Summary:
   A new parent describes the love felt when embracing a child for the
   first time, and the feeling that all creation is welcoming the baby, too.
Identifiers: LCCN 2018047888 (print) | LCCN 2018052821 (ebook) |
   ISBN 9780310766575 | ISBN 9780310766698 (hardcover) |
   ISBN 9780310766599 (board book)
Subjects: | CYAC: Stories in rhyme. | Babies--Fiction. | Nature--Fiction.
Classification: LCC PZ8.3.N345 (ebook) | LCC PZ8.3.N345 Won 2019 (print) |
   DDC [E]--dc23

LC record available at https://lccn.loc.gov/2018047888

Design: Ron Huizinga

Printed in China

19 20 21 22 23 24 25 /DSC/ 20 19 18 17 16 15 14 13 12 11 10 9 8 7 6 5 4 3 2 1

Written by Glenys Nellist • Illustrated by Aurelie Blanz

THE WONDER THAT IS YOU

ZONDERkidz

It felt as if the world stood still

The day my dream came true,

And all creation paused to see

The wonder that is you.

It seemed as though the stars smiled down

And twinkled in delight.

And peeked into my arms to see

This precious, perfect sight.

I closed my eyes as sunlight danced

On everything around,

And all creation held its breath

In case you made a sound.

I thought I heard the trees clap hands
And as their leaves unfurled,
They whispered softly in the breeze,
Welcome to our world.

Each flower nodded in the wind

And waved to say *hello*.

They knew you were a special one

And wanted you to know.

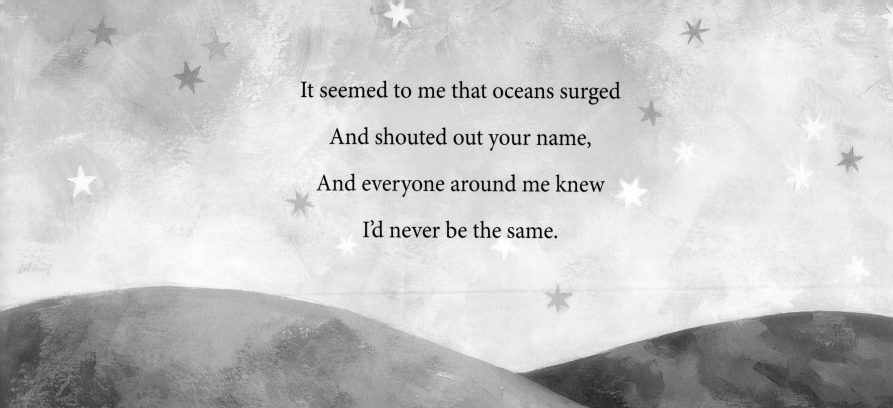

It seemed to me that oceans surged

And shouted out your name,

And everyone around me knew

I'd never be the same.

And could it be that every bird

Sang loud from every tree,

A melody to celebrate

The gift you were to me?

And all the rivers in the woods

Just chuckled as they ran

And bubbled over with the news

The day your life began.

And did I dream the silver moon

That sparkled high above,

And murmured, *Little One, you're here!*

Let's wrap you up in love?

I almost thought my heart would burst

With all the love inside.

And I just could not hold it in,

No matter how I tried.

It felt as if my love took flight

And soared into the air,

And joined creation's welcome song

As you were lying there.

I held you close while all the world

Was hushed to let you sleep,

From meadow, hill, and mountain high

To streams and oceans deep.

And then I knew you were the one

Whom I was meant to hold,

And every day since you arrived

Your story would be told.

It felt as if the world stood still

The day my dream came true,

And all creation paused to see . . .

The wonder that is you.